S0-DOP-634

We Are Whoooo We Are

May you become whoooo you are meant to be!
Melinda S Chambers

Melinda Chambers

illustrated by
Sue Ann Maxwell Spiker

Terra Alta, WV

We Are Whoooo We Are

by Melinda Chambers

illustrated by Sue Ann Maxwell Spiker

Second Printing July 2007
Third Printing February 2015

To order additional copies of this book or for book publishing information, or to contact the author:

Headline Kids
P. O. Box 52
Terra Alta, WV 26764

Tel: 800-570-5951
Email: mybook@headlinebooks.com
www.headlinebooks.com
www.headlinekids.com
www.MelindaChambers.com

Published by Headline Books
Headline Kids is an imprint of Headline Books

ISBN 0-929915-46-1
ISBN-13: 978-00929915-46-3

Library of Congress Control Number: 2006934025

PRINTED IN THE UNITED STATES OF AMERICA

Dedicated to
grandchildren—
yours and mine.

Ribbons of light filtered through the darkness as the great horned owl returned to his forest perch in the massive oak tree. Watching for his return, the owlet pranced on the limb, eager to hear of his father's latest adventures. After feeding the owlet a few morsels of food from his hunt, the father owl stretched his wings, yawned, and settled in for a peaceful snooze, since that is what great horned owls do during the day.

Disappointed in the lack of conversation from his father, the owlet moved closer to him on the limb. Full of questions, the young owlet began, "Why can't we sleep at night and hunt in the daytime?"

The owl smiled as he remembered a long time ago he had posed the same question to his father. "Because, son, that's what great horned owls do. We hunt at night and rest during the day."

"But why?"

The sleepy owl, annoyed with the questions, answered simply, "Because we are WHOOOO we are." With that said, he closed his eyes and pretended to sleep.

The owlet didn't mind his father sleeping, but with the sun peeping through to where he was perched, his large eyes got even bigger. In the distance he heard, "Caw...Caw...Caw." His saucer-like eyes looked upward as he nudged his father with his wing. "What was that?"

His father realized his morning nap was now out of the question. "That's a crow, which is nature's wake-up call to tell forest creatures that it's time to get up...unless you're an owl and they're telling you it's time to go to bed," the owl added with a bit of sarcasm.

By now the forest was awakened. Birds were busy feeding their young and nature's sounds were abundant. The owlet wondered how anyone could possibly sleep through all this excitement, as he shot a questioning "eye" on his father.

Just then the owlet's attention was averted to the forest floor where he saw a bird with his head cocked. "What could he possibly be listening for?"

1

"That is the robin and she is listening for earthworms that are moving just below the surface of the ground. Many of the forest's birds have excellent hearing, just like we do. When the robin hears the worm, she dives down and pulls it up from the ground. She then chews it up and feeds it to her hungry brood."

"Yuck!"

"Sorry, son," the owl laughed. "I didn't mean to spoil your appetite. But robins are great nurturers. They stay very busy finding fruit, bugs, and even worms to feed their young."

"Just like you and mom keep me well fed."

"Yes, that's why you're growing so fast!"

With that, the owlet stretched his head, puffed out his chest, and began to hoot. All of a sudden he heard an echo that sounded just like him, but of course it couldn't be. The owlet's eyes got great big (even bigger than they already were) and he exclaimed, "WHOOOO was that?"

The great horned owl turned his mighty head behind him so he could see where the sound was coming from. "Look on that maple tree. That's a mockingbird mimicking the sound you just made."

"How did he do that? Listen...now he's making noises like other birds I've heard. I wish I could do that," the owlet said wistfully.

"Yes, mockingbirds have beautiful songs, but they don't come up with those songs themselves. They just repeat everything they hear as though it were their own ideas. Why, those mockingbirds haven't had an original thought since I've known them!"

His curiosity now at a peak, the owlet asked, "Then WHOOOO has the best voices in the forest?"

After several minutes of silence, the owl answered, "There are many beautiful voices in the forest, but one of my favorite is the sparrow's. In fact, there's one on that mountain laurel."

"You mean that tiny little bird with the drab feathers can sing?"

"You have a lot to learn, son, but as you get older you'll find that there's more to a bird than his feathers. In spite of his small size and dull coloring, the little fellow has one of the prettiest songs you'll ever hear. He seems to enjoy bringing happiness to others through his song."

The owlet, pleased that his father was such a wise owl, nestled close to him and listened to the beautiful songs of the sparrows as he drifted off to sleep.

By now the sun was directly overhead and the warmth of the sun's rays was filtering through the branches of the oak tree. Suddenly the owls were awakened by the feeding sounds of several large birds. Wrinkling his beak in disgust the owlet asked, "What's that smell?"

Not as bothered by the nasty smell as the owlet was, the great horned owl explained that those birds were vultures. "They're nature's garbage collectors. They clean up the messes that are left on the forest floor and help bring cleanliness and order back to the forest."

Closing his weary eyes once again, the owl drifted to sleep. The peaceful moment was disturbed, however, by the owlet's excited chattering. "What is it, now?" asked the owl.

"Look over there! It's beautiful! What is it?"

Squinting his tired eyes, the owl was able to see the bird on a distant limb. "This is indeed our lucky day, son. That's a bluebird. Some people call it the bluebird of happiness. It's pretty to look at, has a sweet song, and is useful to the forest since it eats so many insects that would otherwise damage the forest's foliage. Glad we didn't miss it."

"That's for sure," chimed in the owlet. "We would have missed it if we had been asleep!" he added slyly. Then the owlet began to dance around the limb, nearly falling off.

"What's gotten into you?"

"I can't help myself! Seeing that bluebird just makes me want to dance around this limb."

"Well, remember WHOOOO you are," said the owl.

The owlet took a deep, huffy breath as he gained his composure. In fact, he had almost calmed down when he heard loud screeching coming from the tree in front of them.

"Don't move," said the owl. "Those are blue jays."

"I see them," said the stiffened owlet. "Wow! They're really beautiful! Their feathers are much prettier than mine. I'll bet the rest of the birds like hanging around the blue jays."

"Only those who don't know any better," snapped the owl.

"Why do you say that?"

"Well, son, looks can only go skin deep. The blue jays like to terrorize the smaller birds and to tear down what they've worked so hard to build."

J
Big J

"I guess looks can be deceiving, huh?"

"Yes, son, you're getting wiser by the minute."

By now it was evening in the forest and the sun's light was beginning to fade, causing dark shadows to fall on the oak's branches. There was a faint coo, coo sound of a mourning dove in the distance as the owl once again began to prepare for his nightly prowl. "The dove you hear in the distance is nature's way of saying that all is well in the forest. Some people call it the dove of peace."

"Thanks for answering so many of my questions today. I can hardly wait until tomorrow when I can discover more things about the forest."

"Whoa, son, an owl has to sleep sometime."

"I know. I remember. We are WHOOOO we are, just like all of the birds we saw today."

Suddenly a twig snapped on the forest floor as a young boy walked by the massive oak. The owl, busy preening his feathers, stopped for a moment until the boy was out of sight.

"WHOOOO was that?" the owlet whispered in his father's ear.

"That strange creature is a boy. He's part of a group called 'people'."

"So, then, are people like birds...they are WHOOOO they are?"

"No, that's the odd thing. They can choose WHOOOO they want to be. In fact, they can choose to be like several birds. They can bring happiness like the bluebird, say nice things like the sparrow, be nurturers like the robin, keep order like the vultures, and even promote peace like the dove. But they can also choose to spread rumors like the mockingbirds or be bullies like the blue jays."

"Gee, people are so lucky. Say, if they can choose WHOOOO they want to be, then I'll bet there aren't any mockingbirds or blue jays in the people world."

"Well, son, that's the strangest thing of all...," he said as he flew into the night sky.

About the Author

Melinda Spiker Chambers grew up in the rural mountains of central West Virginia in Lewis County. She received her BS from West Virginia University and MS from Ohio State University. Besides being an educator, she also writes an award-winning column, *Homespun*, for the *Hampshire Review*, and is active with both her church and community.

Melinda is a Mom's Choice Award Winning author and is part of the Headline Kids School Show Program. She visits schools, libraries, Parent/Teacher Organizations, and conducts workshops.

Melinda is married to Byron K. Chambers, a retired law enforcement captain with the WV Division of Natural Resources. Together they have two children, Kelly and Chris, and several grandchildren. Raised to have an appreciation for natural beauty, Melinda enjoys looking for the lessons that nature so abundantly teaches to those who take the time to listen.

About the Illustrator

Sue Ann Maxwell Spiker is known for her ability to capture nature's beauty through her watercolor paintings. A native West Virginian, Sue Ann was raised in Doddridge County and currently lives on a farm in Jane Lew with her husband, Dr. John Spiker. Sue Ann graduated from Glenville State College with a BA in art education. She and her husband have four children, Jonelle, John, Byron, and David, and several grandchildren. Besides working on the farm, Sue Ann and her husband also own and operate Sunny Pointe Guest House.